THIS IS
(not about)
DAVID
BOWIE

FJ Morris

ISBN: 978-1-9164483-0-8 paperback
ISBN: 978-1-9164483-1-5 ebook

Retreat West Books
https://retreatwestbooks.com

CONTENTS

Part One

*'I always had a repulsive need
to be something more than human…
I want to be superhuman.'*

– David Bowie

When David Bowie moved in

David Bowie moved in when Sarah and Caleb had their backs to each other. It wasn't obvious at first. David left his Union Jack coat hanging on the peg in the hallway.

'Whose coat is that?' said Caleb.

'Looks like David Bowie's,' said Sarah.

'Don't be daft. Whose is it?'

Sarah had no answers for him; just a load of eyebrow raises and shoulders that hunched up as if they were pinched by pegs on a washing line. Caleb tried to decode her, tried to work out her next move, hoping she'd send out her real thoughts in an unknown code. But they were too encrypted. Locked.

Pieces of Bowie landed daily. It was strategic at first. Nothing was replaced. Only the gaps were filled, the things that were missing: a chess set, a record player, dancing shoes. Sarah put on the red shoes and tapped across the black and white tiles on the kitchen floor to Al Green.

'Is he moving in?' said Caleb.

'Not that I know of.'

'We don't have room for all his stuff.'

'What does it matter? You like Bowie, don't you?'

'I love Bowie. That's the problem.'

Caleb made a quiet move, manoeuvring the red shoes into the cupboard. But Bowie showed up when Caleb stayed late at work. Sarah played chess with him. He sacrificed his pawns so that she could corner him. They laughed and danced on the kitchen's chess-board floor, moving as rooks, sliding forward three squares, one across. Not once in opposition.

Caleb noticed Sarah's hands were free now. They weren't tucked into her corners: her pockets, her armpits. They were fanning signals and signs that he could read. So he let it go on, and he sat at dinner with the three of them eating mac 'n cheese. And he thought they could do it, the three of them together, that Bowie would fill the gaps.

But Caleb's toothbrush went missing. Then his books vanished, one by one. His favourite painting that they'd picked out on their honeymoon was now an empty white square on the wall.

'I never liked that one anyway,' said Sarah.

And it was as if he was being knocked out, pieces of

him were being taken. He was used to playing with Sarah, but he couldn't compete with Bowie.

So when he found his shoes heading out the front door, he forfeited. There was no counterattack, no line of defence. He just grabbed his coat from the peg, stepped into his shoes and didn't look back.

To the woman who saved my life

You never knew.

I sat on a wall with only one way out. Backed onto a ledge with LIARLIARLIAR and SLUTWHOREBITCH going over and over and over at me until I believed it.

You sat next to me with a scar that dripped down by the side of your eye like an everlasting tear. 'You're like a mirror,' you said. 'We've matching scars.'

And you didn't know how I got that scar, you hadn't a clue. You didn't know who did it. Why nobody believed me when I told them. You didn't know they thought I'd done it to myself. You didn't know that I'd spent years trying to hide it with makeup, distract from it with piercings and tattoos.

You had no idea how much I hated being reminded of it every time I looked into the mirror, so much so, that I ended up hating me and became the LIARLIARLIAR SLUTWHOREBITCH until I wasn't worth saving.

But you...

You put your hand on mine and said: 'It's beautiful

on you. Stick with it.'

And I hated you for saying that. I hated you for saying that all of it was beautiful. That everything that had hurt me was anything but ugly. But it was the way that you looked at me. The way that you saw me. You couldn't have known what had happened, but somehow, in some way, you did.

You knew.

There were no stars

apollo 13 was doomed from the outset.

number 13 – unlucky. not a surprise that it got stuffed really. it left at 13:13 CST. far too many thirteens for my liking. and harry was 13 when we watched it fire up into space from our neighbour's house.

'Shoot for the moon; you might get there.' Buzz Aldrin.

APOLLO 13 / april / 11 / 1970: we sit at arms-length from the tv, its antenna yawning up and out, catching the waves coming in. harry shouts LIFT OFF and hits me up the back of the head. he's such a dipshit. but my dream takes off, strapped into a fake-wooden box with a glass screen – a 12-inch CT2217BM Mitsubishi capsule. i have a dream. i now know, without a shadow of a doubt, who i'm going to be.

december / 25 / 1971: our front room is a launch pad. grandma's cigarettes billow like thrusters. i tell her i want to be an astronaut. she laughs and says – does that make you major tom?

then of course harry gets in on it: ha – ground control major! ground control! major tom.

they choke on their laughing.

'We choose to go to the moon in this decade and do the other thing, not because they are easy but because they are hard.'
JFK.

i wasn't done yet. this was the age of dreams. i grew up listening to robin hood and peter pan and j-f-fucking-k. 'come with me, where dreams are born… never grow up.' it was also the age of nixon, protests, broken beatles, but also the bluest of skies – the first concord, the first jumbo jet, the first robot on the moon and venus. the world was opening up. dreams were becoming possibilities.

APOLLO 13 / april / 14 / 1970: a whole 56 hours go by with no major event. But when they reach 200,000 miles from earth, an oxygen tank explodes. the command service module is powered down. only the lunar module can support their lives. there are men with plastic models on CBS explaining to nations the gravity of the situation. houston's mission control room is buzzing over and over and over and over. there are press conferences. animations.

december / 25 / 1972 / 18:00: nobody says anything about the empty chairs but they're all I can look at. grandma goes on about apollo. that it aint real. it's all a show. it's all puppets and movie sets down in florida. how on earth can they get live footage from the moon? i can't even call your aunt carol in toronto. aint real, she says. but harry tells her that he'll show her, that he's gunna be an astronaut, better than anyone, and he'll bring a piece of the moon back just for her. she buys him a gi joe astronaut and apollo rocketship after that. harry was an ass, no doubting that, but he was a smart ass. cunning too. he had the charms to make anyone believe he could do anything. i didn't.

APOLLO 13 / april 15 / 1970: the crippled spacecraft continues to the moon, circles it, and begins a long, cold journey back to earth. nobody on the flight is going to touch the moon. the dream is over.

harry and i both went to air cadets. but i failed the eye tests and the medical. my eyes or my brain, who knows what… can't see colours right and i wonder what i'm seeing when everyone is seeing something else. what am i missing? so my dream becomes like the empty chairs at christmas, and i can't stop looking at the empty space, the vast, empty, wide-open absence of life. there were no stars. only a vacuum. i wasn't going to be an astronaut.

not for harry though… that motherfucker went on to be a fighter pilot. call it what you will. delusional. whatever. but i had dreams and harry stole them.

APOLLO 13 / april / 17 / 1970: the countdown to earth begins. will the heat shield stay intact? will they make it? miss logan, who always said watching TV gives you square eyes, rolls out the box into class and says we're living through history and we should all pay attention because we're all going to have to write an essay on it. there's a man on the tv, waiting. he chews on his crossed fingers. and i think how weird it is that he has them crossed, right? how a man his age and with his smarts believes in something unexplained. but i guess despite all the maths, all the calculations, all the measurements, and talent and whatnot – man had only luck now. that was it…

stupid

damn

luck.

there are sailors on USS iwo jima who look to the skies. on the tv there are men watching on portable ones. tvs on tvs on tvs on tvs on tvs and on tvs forever and ever. Radio black out. 4 minutes, come and go. there is nothing.

i didn't speak to harry for years when he stole my life. i don't know what happened in between. there was just more of that black stuff, more of that wide open space, floating. and i didn't want to look into it. i didn't want to be faced with what it was. but it didn't matter. it's always sat at the kitchen table with me, eating me away.

'The moon is moving away from the earth at a rate of 3.78 centimeters / 1.5 inches per year.
One day, we will lose it entirely.'

april / 11 / 1979: i left earth for the first time and didn't even realise it. i woke up at 13:13 pm in an empty drive-in car lot with no clue as to where or what, and barely who i was, and i totally freak out. i tell harry but he just laughs and says: ground control major!

no one ever believes me. this isn't how i wanted to see the stars.

'They're travelling over the backside of the moon now. Our velocity reading here is 7777 feet per second. Now we're in our period of the longest wait, continuing to monitor this at Apollo control, Houston. No contact yet, we're standing by…'

i get flash backs at night. the greys have me on a table. they've got my eyes pulled open and looking into them – their eyes are black holes of nothing that i can't escape. i begin to notice that i would get this tingling sensation before i got abducted, before i blacked out and woke up in random places all over town. but they never abandoned me completely. they would always get me home some-how. once i got accustomed to the thought, i realised how incredible it was that i got to go further than any apollo mission had. further than any man could get me.

APOLLO 13 / april / 16 / 12:07 pm: men fall from the skies. they drop into the pacific ocean like those tiny plastic, parachuting soldiers. i see them fall fall fall fall from space. so peaceful. protected in their capsule. they had been the farthest any man had ever been. and as i kick the empty desk chair in front of me and miss logan gives me the eye, i wonder why they bothered coming back.

'I'm coming back in… and it's the saddest moment of my

life.' Ed White, first American spacewalk, 3 June 1965.

april / 16 / 2004: i thought of gi joe when they found harry... the one grandma got him. it was blonde like he was. had this white jumpsuit and a dog tag that, when you pulled it, he talked to you. there were different marks on the cord and if you pulled it to a long one he'd say something different, like: we have ignition... lift off! but harry yanked it so hard that joe was speechless and the cord never rolled back in, so he hung joe from the kitchen light one day, boot missing, swaying in the breeze coming through the screen door. that's how i see harry now... swinging, boot missing. orbited by empty chairs.

and i can't shake it. the emptiness of it. what rotten luck he had, and how damn terrible it was for him that he never got to go to outer space,

that this was the only way he could get off this planet...

to see stars.

Saving Superman

- How many people did you try and save today?
- *Three.*
- And did you save anyone?
- *No.*
- What happened?
- *They kept telling me to piss off.*
- Right.
- *Except one lady. But she wasn't really drowning.*
- How do you know?
- *She was sitting in a pond that was knee-deep. She could have just walked out.*
- And you left her?
- *Yes.*
- Good. You're making progress.
- *But three people still died.*
- Are you sure about that?
-

- Clark?
- *Yes?*
- If you couldn't save anybody, what then?
- *Well, I wouldn't be Superman.*
- You'd be Clark Kent. Is that not enough?
- *Clark is a loser. A geek. I'd rather be Superman.*
- Why?
- *Because he's strong. Powerful. Confident and admired.*
- But why can't Clark be those things?
- *Clark is… Superman but with kryptonite. Human. Powerless. He can't save anyone.*
- Neither can Superman.
- *He can.*
- Who? Who does Superman save?
- *He saves Clark.*
- He saves you? How?
- *He makes Clark worth saving.*

Is there life on Mars?

The eve of war

'With infinite complacency men went to and fro over this globe about their little affairs, serene in their assurance of their empire over matter.'

War of the Worlds by H.G. Wells.

No one would have believed that, in the middle of the 21st century, my love could kill you. We had taken so much for granted. There was a thickness to the air that evening, which seemed to coagulate in front of me. It felt more of a presence than a space. I figured a storm was coming. I told myself it would be good for the plants. When have we ever let a bit of weather change our plans? It would pass.

But what I wasn't to know was that we were being invaded. That silently, ancient forces were forever changing, moving and spreading, in a way that was undetected by us. That they waited, biding their time until their collaborative strength could overpower us. We were sitting prey.

You came for dinner. An irony that I cannot avoid, that I cannot help but say in poor taste because I know it would have made you laugh. It was not an evening like any other. Unknown to you, I had planned to tell you how I felt about you. This wasn't the first time. I had chickened-out when we went to the cinema a few weeks before. The gore in the film's action scenes had spoiled the moment.

'They were too life-like,' you said. 'Who wants a virtual reality like that? I'll get PTSD at this rate. Bloody eejits!'

You longed for days that you were never born in. Films that were far away and flat. You always said – "Isn't life enough without forcing yourself through that?" And you had more stuff than anyone I'd ever met, most of which didn't work.

You liked to touch real things.

'I feel like I can count on them being there,' you said. 'Like you, I don't want to touch your Calling-Avatar – it's not the same. It's missing something. Probably something so microscopic about you that nobody or nothing could pick it up, could even be aware of. Something invisible.'

You were right as always. Simulations made everyone

look better than they were: smoothing out lines and bags under our eyes, knowing that we'd rather look better. It didn't care that I wanted to see you, touch you, the *real* you. In your curly hair, there was a patch of almost straight, soft hair, but your Calling-Avatar always curled it out of existence. It was a secret piece of you that I loved to twirl with my finger. When you arrived for dinner that night, I ran my fingers through your hair to find it, to check it was you.

'Is that for me?' you asked.

My fear rose. I was ready, aimed and loaded with words to say, but before I could take a breath deep enough, my unforeseen weapon had already drawn blood. Small. Tiny. A wound on your hand that took more blood that it deserved. I scrambled for the spray-on-plaster, washed out your palm, and when the wound closed up, so had I.

In that moment, little did I know how much it all mattered. How small seconds would play out. How tiny bits of time would derail us both. That if I hadn't been so assured in our empire of matter, in my disbelief of our mortality, that if when I ran my fingers through your hair I'd found only curls, you'd have been safe.

Part Two

In 1970, when Bowie briefly formed
the band The Hype,
everyone who was in the band
dressed up as a super hero.
They were booed off the stage
everywhere
they went.

The trial of Mr Travers

A courtroom. When the curtain rises, there is a judge sat on a platform behind a plinth. He's upstage centre, facing the audience. Mrs Travers is centre-right stage in a dock. She is in her sixties and dressed as David Bowie's Ziggy Stardust. She has short red hair, red lips, and a round circle drawn on her head. Her expression doesn't change throughout.

One large, single spotlight fills the stage like a bright tunnel of light. Mr Travers is downstage-left with his back to the audience. You cannot see his face, but his greying hair indicates he is in his early forties. He's wearing a suit.

Travers: But she's pretending to be somebody she isn't. *(Points aggressively at Mrs Travers)*

Judge: *(Leans forward)* Who isn't? What are you trying to say, Mr Travers?

Travers: Well, she isn't David Bowie your honour. Can't you see that? Can't anybody see that? (Loudly) She's my mum.

Judge: Mr Travers, we know she isn't David Bowie. She wants to be David Bowie. There's a big difference. What's the harm in that?

Travers: *(Paces)* Well if she was a proper mum. Herself. If she was just my mum. Then I wouldn't be like this. I would have been better. I wouldn't have done what I did.

Judge: *(Angrily)* But she is not on trial, Mr Travers.

Travers: I know, I know. But. I just know that if I had grown up in a normal environment… If she'd just have…

Judge: Did she neglect you, Mr Travers?

Travers: *(Stops pacing)* No.

Judge: Abuse you? Abandon you?

Travers: No, but she did…

Judge: She is not on trial, Mr Travers. *(Points at him)* You were.

Travers: *(Pause)* Were?

Judge: But you were already pardoned before the trial began.

Travers: What?

Judge: *(Shouts)* Pardoned, Mr Travers. You've already been pardoned.

Travers: But I... What about what I did?

Judge: *(Sits back, a little fed up)* Your sentence has been paid in full.

Travers: Paid?

Judge: Yes.

Travers: By who?

Judge: Why... who do you think?

Travers: I don't know...

Judge: You are free to go.

Travers: But... *(looks side to side for reassurance)*

Judge dismisses him with his hand and a voice calls out 'All rise'. The spotlight floods the stage in a flash of blinding light. When it fades, nobody is left but you.

Shrinking giants

I adopted an orphaned giant. He ate custard for breakfast and twirled swings into knots. On the hilltop next to our house, with his hands stuffed into his pockets, he raised his coat above his head and ran around screaming, trying to catch the wind.

Each day he grew and grew, heading for the sky. So I let him go barefoot into puddles of mud to soak up the calcium, so he could branch up, and out. But one day he stopped. Just like that. He didn't budge another inch.

I asked him why, but he just shrugged and said maybe that was it for him. That was as tall as he was going to be. So he traded the sun for LCDs, spending days, hours and minutes signing into screens. I brought a bowl of custard to his room, but it went cold, a yellow skin wrinkling on top.

But you love custard, I said.

Not anymore, he said, that stuff's for kids.

I told myself that he'll start growing again in the spring. But that's when I noticed him shrink. He wasn't ducking to get through doorways anymore. So I asked what was wrong, but my orphan boy said he was fine.

But he wasn't.

He was getting smaller every day. I watched him through the crack in his door, transcribing pre-approved thoughts onto the keyboard. A box popped up: a new conversation. If I hadn't been blinking, I could've sworn I saw him shrink by an inch at least. So I went peeking into places I shouldn't be and into conversations I wasn't in, and between the words filled with Zs instead of Ss, it was there. I saw what made my boy shrink. It was a slaughter-house of syllables, letters and words as blades and knives, cutting him down, shredding him into pieces. All aimed at a human being. My human being. My son.

I took him to our hilltop, the one where he used to fly. But he sat on a rock, limp as a willow. He asked me why we were there, and I told him that I used to come to this hilltop with a giant once. A giant orphan boy, bigger than any boy I ever knew.

I sat down and reached for him in all the ways I could. I told him I knew what had been happening, and as I pulled on his arm, I saw his wounds, his self-pruning. He crumpled, and sap rolled down his cheeks.

What do you mean? He said, pulling his arm away.

But he didn't shrivel from me as I entwined my hand in his and told him about the first day I saw him. He was the biggest baby of the bunch. I could barely hold him in my arms, but my love for him was gigantic and would wrap around him a hundredfold. And with that, he whispered to me: But you're the only one, Mum. You're the only one.

Tuning in

Ryan's my default station. He's who I wake up with every morning. But people tune-in when I'm Ryan. You can put on a suit that's all like James Brown, Sinatra and shit, and you're the boss. Part the air waves! That's all good, but it ain't enough. Like, who listens to one station their whole lives and doesn't get sick of it?

I started tuning-in to Yvonne when I was in high school. There was so much of me that wanted to come out, but like, couldn't, not as Ryan. I wanted my nipples to be like dials that could be turned up so that my flat chest would pop out, loud. I wanted heels to strut, and eyelashes that could dust the ceiling.

All those rules! You can't cry. You can't wear a skirt. You can't giggle. You can't be sensitive. Absolutely no make-up. You can't back out of a fight. You can't be a weak sissy-boy or you're done for.

But the rules for women are background noise. You can't wear your skirt too high. You can't wear too much make-up or grind on someone, otherwise you're asking for it. And they will take it.

I'm a man, but not man enough. My Dad taught me that much. Here's the line, Ryan. Don't step over that line, Ryan. Blokes are always measured:

I'm all bad-ass and sass until someone pokes my inflated chest and tells me they're too big or too small, and find myself being measured, again:

By height   By waist
By shoe size   By boob size

By hand size

Which will tell you my you-know-what size,

Because no matter who I choose to be,
people are obsessed about what's down there.
Any deviation and you don't qualify. You don't make
the grade.
Not even fit for radio, they'll say. Like that's all
that matters.

'Pick a side,' they all requested.
But being a man and woman like totally sucked:
a whole bunch of plastic rulers and scales ready to trip you
up, bad.
I wanted to evolve into something better, like step outside
the frequencies.

That's when I tuned-in to Bowie.
Bowie is static noise. The in-between. Not to be tuned.
People totally couldn't understand it when I said I
was both.
They tuned-out when I said: 'I'm non-binary,' til I said,
'I'm David Bowie'.
They accepted that. They could always accept
David Bowie.
I'm not David Bowie...
But then again, nobody ever was.

Loving the alien

My heart turned cold over the popping bubbles in the sink. I stood there, a palm on my chest, the cold bleeding into my fingers. The pain was crisp, like submerging into liquid nitrogen. But there was no steam for me. My heart had to be pumping hot for that. The promoter was microscopic; the tiniest of word-sequences. But they always are. At first, I'd hoped it was a glitch and that my heart would thaw in the afternoon sun, or after dinner, or by the end of the week. I strapped hot water bottles around me, drank tea, watched heart-warming films, but nothing worked.

I thought I was lucky that nobody could see it. But I was wrong. This wasn't symptomatic. It wasn't a sickness that would go away. It was genetic; an alien gene in my very DNA. Not long after, my blood ran cold too. My son reached for my hand and pulled away. 'Cold hands, warm heart,' I said, more to myself than to him. My husband kicked me away under the duvet. 'You're too cold,' he said, and I was.

I hoped and prayed that my heart would spark and spring to life again. But when our Little John came to our room in tears, he asked for his daddy, and the tongue in my mouth flicked out between pointed teeth. And I was so ashamed, mortified even, that I didn't speak after that unless my back was turned.

Silence followed, and then scales. They were dull grey. I thought I'd slept on a pumpkin seed, but when I picked it off, it bled. More followed. I scratched them off in the shower at first, bleeding purple into the plug hole. But it couldn't last. They were coming in thick and fast. People were going to see it soon, my heart on my sleeve, frozen cold. They would see what I had become.

My husband noticed first. I wrapped myself up in reasons, blaming it on the weather, him, work, the weather again, God, my dead mother, my super-sister with five kids, the next door neighbour's voices that came through the wall, the city, hormones, my age, not being able to have any more children, and then, just when I thought I had more excuses to come, I had none.

He didn't say anything.

He sent me to hell in a stare, picking out his beard hair, squinting. He pulled his lips in, the way he does when he smells dirty nappies. He was glancing over every scab and every scale I couldn't scrub off. How my eyes had become black holes. He had a million ideas that could fix me, and I pretended that they could work, that my genome was pure, untouched, human.

But nothing worked. My eyes were blank and unblinking. His gaze switched poles, pushing away from mine when I drew near. 'I'm not sure it's safe for John to be around you,' he said.

And he was right. I wouldn't have a heartless alien near him either. I stood at the door, a green-grey shadow with no bags, ready to leave. But something inside of me knocked over, spilled out, foul and messy.

'I'm glad,' I said, drawing a deep breath, a run up. 'That we couldn't have another.'

He tilted his head. 'Another what?'

I nodded to Little John's picture framed in wood.

'Well,' he said. 'It's good we didn't bring another child into this.'

'No, I mean. I've always been glad.'

'What?'

'I didn't want another,' I said, and I wasn't sure what made me say it, or why I hadn't said it before, earlier, way earlier than now.

'But what about... you cried for days after.'

'From shame.' I felt a bubbling in my stomach, a warming in my veins. 'I didn't grieve for her. I just felt...'

I threw my hand over my mouth. I should have kept it buried. Good people don't say these things; they don't think or feel these things. Good people love their children.

'No,' he said, grabbing my arm and pulling it, scales falling to the floor like coins. 'Say it.'

My heart broke in two, spilling out fire and pain and heat through me. It melted the ice until it ran down my face. 'Relief,' I said, my voice cracking like burning wood. 'I felt relief.'

He stepped back. His face was shock and horror, frozen. 'But why?'

I shook my head, but I could feel my heart beating again, throwing itself against me, pummelling me until the numbing cold became sore. I felt something again. 'I don't know.'

He didn't move; he just stared at the floor. He'd gone in, away from me and into himself. 'Jim?' I said.

He looked up at me with slow blinks and murky stares. 'Your eyes. They're not holes anymore.'

'Do you hate me?'

He pulled away. 'I...' he sighed. 'No, I don't. Look,

let's go sit down and talk about this.'

He took my hand, but his was cold and clammy, and when his eyes caught the light, his pupil narrowed into a slice of darkness, and I knew then, that he was lying to me.

Is there life on Mars?

The fighting begins

'And now, fought with the terrible weapons of super-science, menacing all mankind and every creature on the Earth comes the War of the Worlds.'

It was difficult to see how sick you were on account of all the calling-filters. But you listed your symptoms to me: aching, then fever, then chills, then fever, then chills. You told me not to come over just in case it was contagious. Your home health sensors alerts went off, and they were sending over a medical professional the next day. You told me not to worry.

You started to make a list. What were the things I had always wanted to do? What were the things we should go and do together? You said you wanted to see things for real: the Pyramids, the Great Wall of China, Mars.

I laughed. They've been talking about the Mars programme for decades, it'll never happen. Not for the likes of you and me. Anyway, you wouldn't want to go to

Mars, there's nothing there. Not a single flower or tree. It's not for humans.

I should have seen through it: the list. You didn't tell me then that you already knew you were untreatable. That making the list was to give you hope, so that you could keep on fighting. If I'd have known, I would have said better things. I would've given you hope for other worlds, for planets other than this where we aren't losing our place. I would have told you Mars was ours. Together, you and I, forever.

Part Three

*'Aging is an extraordinary process
where you become the person
you always should have been.'*

– David Bowie

Blooming scars

When the David Bowie tattoo bloomed on her chest, she knew what it meant. She doesn't do tattoos. Half-a-dozen piercings and an undercut, sure, but a permanent scar injected under her skin, no thanks. Nope. But this had been a long time coming out.

Bowie's face was haloed in petals, making him a flower. But when she touched him, the skin was raw. He went with her to the hospital. *Not long*, they said. *Not long. Say your goodbyes.* But she hadn't come for that. The skin on her chest popped, twisted and wriggled as she stared at her mother who was pierced with needles, and tattooed with bruises. Bowie was waking up.

'Muv.'

'Sophia.' Her mother's eyes sliced open. 'What *is* that?'

'Tattoo.'

'S'horrible. Why do that to yourself?'

Sophia had so many things she wanted to say to her, so many questions that were hushed and zipped away into the shadows between her ribs, but she couldn't get them out. She was losing her last chance. She felt a bite in her chest, and looked down to see Bowie gazing up, his face reddening. She wanted to hide him, but her mother saw him and disgust scabbed on her face.

'You should have believed her,' said Bowie.

Her mother stared at her, then at Bowie, and back. 'Believe what? What *is* that? What's he talking about?'

'About Uncle Ant,' he said. Sophia's chest swelled out towards her mother. 'You'd have believed Natasha. Why not her? Why don't you love Sophia like her?' Bowie whispered these questions, the questions that Sophia only asked herself in the darkness, the questions that hid behind her thoughts, behind her every blink.

Her mother peeled her face away. 'I don't remember.'

'You invited him in. Even after,' Bowie said.

Her mother glanced back at them, fingers stitched together. 'He was a good man. You were always rebelling with your short skirts and...' She gasped. Monitors stabbed the air with beeps.

'You blame me? You thought it was my fault? I was eleven. If my skirts were too short that was your fault Muv.' Bowie and Sophia spoke together now.

'You were not eleven.'

'You wrote me off, like a car wreck. Too much damage. Not worth the repairs. You owe me a tow truck. You owe me your blood and tears, and scars. You owe it to me to look into my face, Muv! Did it not break you, what he did to me? How did it not break you?'

Sophia was loud, raised up and soaking in the air. Bowie's voice had gone. It was only hers now. Alone. Rough. Broken. Bowie's face was fading from her chest, evaporating, lifting from her. Everyone around was staring. Everyone had heard her. Everyone it would seem, except her mother. Her face was still set, looking away. Cast in denial.

'I am so much more than what happened to me. I am going to be so much more than a survivor. So much more than you, Muv,' Sophia said. 'I know why you've hated me. I forgave you. All that denial, I know it was easier than the truth. And you couldn't face that. Couldn't accept it.'

A single tear oozed from her mother like an infection.

'Do yourself a favour,' Sophia said. 'Let it heal over, for god sake. Forgive yourself before it's too late.' And as Sophia walked away for the last time, she reached for Bowie on her chest to find only her heartbeat, blooming in a rhythm like never before.

Side A
To my daughter

Side B
who I'll never meet

I sent you pieces of me. Did you get them? I'm sorry about the watermarks on Hunky Dory.

I wanted to write to you in kisses and tears, to have them say to you…

something more.

Because my heart only speaks in song and sobs. And I thought that you might recognise their pattern, your DNA spiralled in salt across Bowie's face. Crystallised regret.

But I know better.

And I'm running out of Bowie records: the pieces of me that I want you to have, that I know you'll need, because these my daughter, they were the best of me.

The very best.

And I'm holding the last to my chest so tight. I want the

beatbeatbeat of my heart to groove into the flat, black sun, ready to be spun so that you'll hear me. Please tell me that you hear me? And in the rise and fall of my chest, I remember we only had five years, of kooks and me whispering to you. And I still do, I still do…

I believe in you.

You'll probably think nothing of it; Bowie on your doorstep. You won't think of me, and why would you? But with stars and space and Major Tom, I bring my offering to leave on your altar, the last piece of me. And it's a broken shard.

But it's all I have left of me.

I leave it on your concrete step and I hear a gentle strum muffled by a window pane and I know it so well because it's been on repeat in my head since the day you were born, and it stops me at the gate saying that I won't be sorry if I stay.

And I'm sorry. I am.

Always.

Every.

Time.

But, when I look up at your window and I see a cactus, I know now that it's you.

You are the best of me.

Swings and rocket ships

They call me Grace from space. Mum says my head is somewhere between Neptune and Pluto, like the cartoon dog. My sister loved dogs. We used to sit on swings and jet off into space. We'd push out our legs and snap them back, launching into the sky. On the up, we'd see the moon. Next: Mars. Sometimes Silly Lily would sit backwards to catch the sun and Venus. But most times we'd try to go all the way round, seeing where it might take us. But we never got over the bar.

Then one day, just after our eighth birthday, she did it. Lily went full circle. Alone. She didn't wait for my up-swing. She didn't even say goodbye. Her seat just fell back to earth, empty. It winded me. I tried to follow her, but my legs must've been too small or my lungs had shrunk or something. I was too heavy to get off the ground.

Mum and Dad didn't like me going on the swings after that. She was dead, they said. I had to come back down to earth. But I didn't see why. The stars were a better place to be. But Dad didn't want to lie to me. He'd say: there's nothing else, no after, this is *it*, Grace. But I didn't believe him. I knew Lily went to Pluto. I was sure of it. She didn't disappear into nothing. I'd have felt it. We were locked together you see, like two cogs on a bike. I wouldn't work if she just went poof like that, into nothing.

They made me keep a diary and took me to see Doctor Brown. He said he was an astronaut too, exploring and discovering like me. But he didn't want to go on the swings. He only wanted to talk about my adventures. So I told him of the time me and Lily skated on the rings of Saturn and ate rock cakes on Mars. I told him about the everlasting gobstopper we found on Jupiter and the fart-clouds on Uranus.

He asked me how I felt about her dying. But she wasn't dead. She left. I thought she was selfish to go on her own. We did everything together. She should've taken me with her. I couldn't breathe properly now. It was like she'd punched one of my lungs into a pancake. I didn't know if I'd be able to swing again with one lung and no Flight Commander.

But I did.

A spaceman helped me.

Doctor Brown's eyebrows almost jumped off his head

when I said that. Then they hung over his eyes, crinkling his face into a question mark, and he quizzed me for ages.

'What d'you say?' He spat.

'What?' I said

'About a spaceman.'

'What about it?'

'Who is he?'

I shrugged. 'Dunno. He said he was a spaceman.'

'Where did you meet him?'

'He was sat on Lily's seat on the swing.'

'Do your parents know about this?'

'No, but they don't know anything about space, and he's a spaceman.'

'A Spaceman? What makes you think he's a spaceman?'

'He's got really strong legs and good lungs, so he goes up for miles.'

'But Grace, you can't talk to strangers. You must be careful, remember? Stranger danger? They'll promise you the moon, but really they're out to hurt you.'

'No, he's not like that.'

And it didn't matter how hard I told him about the spaceman's nice face and laugh, or how he skipped with me on Pluto and ran with me to visit Lily on Saturn, or how the people I knew hurt me more than any stranger ever had, Doctor Brown wouldn't listen.

He must have told Mum and Dad, which scared and confused them I think because they knew, like I did, that the swings were in our back garden. So they kept asking if he had a name, or if I'd recognised him from the village or whether he was a made-up-person, and if so, was I lonely? So I had to tell them about the spaceman all over again, but they weren't getting it and they asked too many questions that they didn't give me time to answer, so I shouted over them: THE SPACEMAN COMES FROM OUTER SPACE. HE'S NOT FROM AROUND HERE!

But I think I made it worse, because I had to see Doctor Brown even more after that. They gave me sideway-looks whenever I was being silly. So I had to be serious and quiet and wait. And wait some more…

The spaceman warned me about a day; one where I'd see Mum sat on the swings. He told me that she was planning on cheating, taking a shortcut out of here. And I saw it in her eyes at first. They were hazy, like a nebula was getting in the way of her seeing properly. Then I saw her through the kitchen window, rocking slowly back and forth in the snow. Then she kicked back her legs and started swinging. She fought with the wind. Her eyes burned like a comet with a tail of tears. She was going. I could hear the countdown with each swing:

Five.

Four.

Three.

Two.

I ran out and I screamed. She jammed her feet into the ground, bringing her mission to a halt, and just stared at me with tears dripping down her chin. I told her that she wasn't allowed to go after Lily. What would me and Dad do if Lily and Mum were both living on Pluto? She looked at me as if she was trying to find something she'd lost. She wiped her nose and pulled me in, her arms squeezing me.

'I'm sorry', she said. 'I'm sorry. I love you spacey Gracey. I just wanted to see Lily one more time.'

'We'll go together,' I said, grabbing her hand. 'Only for a visit. The spaceman showed me how. Lily would like that.' And so I sat on the swing next to her, holding her hand to make a seat belt between us, and we started to swing together.

Five.

Four.

Three.

Two.

One.

Lift off.

A song of Space

You tell me that I am nothing,

that I have no heart, no substance,

that I am filled with dark, empty space.

You tell me that I am void,

look through me, try to conquer me,

treat me as if I do not exist.

But you are wrong.

I'm the lungs that empty before a gasp,

the stretch and view of your gaze up,

I am the arms holding supernovas and planets and
     milkyways,

and the eye that watches them play.

I am the spaces between words,

the dichotomy between realms,

I am unanswered questions,

the blink in your eye.

I am the reason the moon can block the sun,

the semicolon between now and then,

between memories and heart beats,

the gap from here to your dreams.

I am the reason you reach,

for a paintbrush, your loved ones,

the reason why you can run,

the reason you are free.

I am the space between,

you and me.

Is there life on Mars?

The Red Weed

'As Man had succumbed to the Martians, so our land now succumbed to the Red Weed...'

You phoned me and when I answered your Calling-Avatar showed up in my living-room. You were in underwear that looked ripe for change and you asked me where you were. Your eyes were misted petri dishes looking through me. You asked me if I was real. If all this, was real. That's when I saw it, your hand was a map of red veins, spreading up your arm like a weed taking over. There was a black hole in your hand, gaping as if someone had taken a bite from you.

'Who did this?' I asked.

'You did,' you said. 'You did.'

I hacked into your health care system while you paced in my living room. You talked about your father, how he was an author called H.G. Wells. But I knew that wasn't true. Your father was a minor, like us. But you insisted.

Talked about him as if he was a prophet. That he foresaw the development of airplanes, tanks, space travel, nuclear weapons, TVs, the internet, invisibility, and bio-engineering.

But he didn't foresee this. Your health record. He didn't foresee that here, in the 21st century, you would be dying from an infection, a war that mankind had already fought and won. A bacterial infection with no antibiotic treatment. He didn't suspect that we would become Martians on our own planet. That we would be next.

The reality hit home, but it was all still virtual. I felt so far away from you, as if a huge gulf was between us. You were in my house, but not really. I wanted to take you to bed, but I couldn't. I wanted to bring you food and drink, but they wouldn't pass your lips.

So I hugged you. So hard. And I reached for the straight tuff of hair in your curls. But it wasn't there.

Part Four

'Everything I've done,
I've done for you.
I move the stars for no one.'

– Jareth, the Goblin King

Ground zero

It ain't his scene, but his mate's new girlfriend, Rachel, drags them into the club anyway. A David Bowie struts onto the stage and the crowd all but lay down their lives for him. He's not even the real thing. But they all have stars in their eyes. He can't stand Bowie. What even *is* he? Just some sort of statement. All style. No substance.

Usually, this sort of stuff doesn't bother him. But this Bowie-bloke in his glitter, skinny trousers, make-up and what-have-you, is digging at his foundations. What's wrong with being a bloke? Does he hate men or something? Weak. That's what he is. First make-up, then what? Where does it end? He's too fat to be Bowie anyhow.

He ditches his mate when the second act comes on, and before he really knows what he's doing, he's pinching Bowie's clothes and running home laughing. He feels like Robin Hood. But when he gets back to his bedsit, still holding them, he tries them on, telling himself it's all down to that whisky he had after that pint. He's in the scaffolds of Bowie and he knows it's all wrong. Why the hell would you want to be Bowie? The clothes feel so small, too tight; too all-out-there and hidden at the same time.

He climbs back into his jeans and Motorhead t-shirt, but now they feel too big, too wide, too much of nothing. The cladding's shoddy; a cowboy job; a composite of his mum and dad. A cobbling-together of ideas that weren't measured or sanded. So the project sagged and has been abandoned by all the women who thought he might be a fixer-upper. Unlike Bowie, not much thought had gone into constructing him.

But building shit is his trade. He could construct something else on these ruins. So he strips off his t-shirt, knocking down the walls his dad had put up; rips off his jeans along with the past his mum had blue-printed. *Pull it all down*, he thought, and so off came his fraying boxers and slacking socks until he's down to ground zero. Brand spanking new. And he struts around over the floorboards in his living room, loving the right-here right-now on his skin, and seeing the past in ruin on the floor. Demolished. And he walks all over them, stamping and singing, thinking he might never put clothes on, ever, again.

Slush puppies

i didn't mean to make up a boyfriend it just happened
when my girl kerry asked me if I was queer and i sorta
panicked cause i wanted to say yes and to tell her how
much i wanted to touch her but the words are gummed
up in my mouth as sticky as toffee so that i chew and
chew on them til im worried my teeth will fall out but
kerry is a ledge with pink hair and bowie posters everywhere and i can get close to her when i talk about my
madeup boyfriend so i show her my school planner where
he writes bowie lyrics to me but what she doesn't know is
that i write them for her and i can almost taste Kerry
when she leans in to read my truth and lies and i know
she would taste sweet like her candyflosshair and my sugar
craving is realbad because im so close to busting out but
she asks me where my boyfriend lives and she wants to
meet him on account of his love of bowie and i panic and
pretend to take her to his house but he isnt there and i tell
her without saying thats because he nowhere and i see
kerry staring at me with eyes like marbled chocolate and

the hunger in me is everything and nothing all at once to the point that when she hugs me goodbye i lose it and i want to absorb every bit of her and i expect her to rip away from my sip and gut me good to tell me to go to hell but she doesn't not one little bit and she turns me into a slush puppy all melting sticky formless as she drinks all of me in

Bunbury snow days

I wanted to be Antonia.

Everyone was freaking out, except her. It like never snows in Bunbury. Bushfires, for sure. That's our bread and butter down-under. But Antonia was like an awesome magnet of coolness. She shaved her head and I swear that even the hair growing back pulled towards her like iron filings. Girls tried to copy her dance routines. Her eyebrows were marker-thick and she wore platform shoes that if I wore them, would look really lame. She stuck silver stars to her temple, and walked with a jean backpack covered with badges. She was perfect.

I wanted to be Antonia. But I didn't have the guts.

When you spoke to her she'd often say 'I'll have to check with David,' or 'David's coming round,' and 'Oh David said it looked good on me too.' Nobody thought much of it. Some best-friend or cousin? But then she came up to me while I was scraping a snowball together, picking out the stones: 'David said I should come talk to you.'

'Really? Why?'

'Dunno. He seemed pretty sure we'd get along. You live far away, don't you? They're closing school early. Do you want to come to mine til your Mom can get you?'

'Yeah alright. Ta.'

I couldn't wait. I followed her out – literally. She always aimed for the fresh snow, to be the one to make the first impression. Her platforms lifted her above it, and I followed in the marks she made. I wanted to be in all of her steps. The snow kept coming but it had no idea where it was going. It was as if pieces from a blank canvas from the past had come to settle in the present, lost, mistaken. In the wrong place at the wrong time.

Antonia's dad was standing by the front door, head up and sticking his tongue out to catch flakes. 'There y'are! Thought you'd gone walkabouts.' He stubbed out his durry and dropped it. 'You were supposed to be back ages ago,' he said.

'Yeah sorry.'

'My gig's cancelled. Watch my kit when you go up.'

We jumped over the hill of cymbals and drum sticks at the bottom of the stairs, and went up to Antonia's bedroom. It was bigger than anything I'd ever seen and even had its own dunny.

'Want to meet David?' she said.

'Uh yeah. Go for it.'

She opened her wardrobe and between the clothes that hung a bit like stage curtains, there was a man-made alien. He had a guitar for a body, CD's for eyes – one blue and one silver, and an old portable CD player for a mouth. Shiny tape ribbon was spilling out of his head, and it was propped on a stool with four giant tapes strapped together for his legs.

'This is David?' I asked.

'Yeah, d'ya like him?'

'Is it a him?'

'Dunno. He's from the moon so he could be anything.'

'What's he doing in your cupboard?'

'Hanging out. We're good mates. Like ET. I look after him. He needs me.'

On the two tapes making up his feet, it said David Bowie, and there was a man with funny hair.

'Why y'looking at his feet?' she asked. I'd never seen her frown before, as if I had stepped on something embarrassing.

'Just wondered where his toes were.'

'What?'

'His toes,' I said. 'He doesn't have any.'

'He doesn't NEED toes,' she shouted. 'Right? He's perfectly fine without them. Nobody needs toes.' She breathed like there was no air.

'I'm sorry,' I said. 'I didn't mean…'

'I don't have toes,' she said.

'What d'you mean?'

'TOES,' she yells. 'I don't have any.' She slid her back down the bedpost and sat on the floor, propped up like a doll.

'Really?'

'Why y'smiling? You're horrible.' She threw her pillow at me, drew in her feet and hugged her knees.

'No, no,' I said and sat next to her. 'It's just…' I took the deepest of breaths, for the deepest of dives. 'I have too many.'

'What? Too many toes?'

'Yeah. More than ten.'

'You do?! Can I see?'

I pulled off my red socks and stretched out my legs, wiggling all my toes, all the normal ones and extra ones.

'Oh my gosh,' she said, and I died inside a little.

'Can I see yours?'

She took off her socks and stretched her feet out next

to mine. They were rounded, forgotten projects, like snowmen beginning to melt.

'David was right,' she said. 'To invite you over. We should be best mates with inside jokes like: *Don't step on my toes*, and then we wink at each other.'

I laughed. 'Wish I could give you some of mine.'

'Toes are lame though, aren't they?'

'I guess.'

Antonia launched up and pressed play on David's mouth. A guitar sound came from two speakers that were his shoulders. She pulled me up with her. Our bare feet facing each other and I felt awesome.

'Maybe we're aliens,' she said. 'Like David.'

Antonia swished her head and air-guitared to a song I had never heard, dancing magic without any toes, and I thought she was probably right. We were total, freakin' aliens, but I still wanted to be Antonia.

Dancing in the street

Tom waits in orbs of lamplight and shields his old Nokia 360 from the rain. But there's no activity, no envelopes, only his message out:

Meet me on Corn Street.
Doesn't matter
what you wear,
just be there x

He's sent this message to a few girls before Hannah but they didn't come, or they turned up only to get him back inside. He checks his phone again—nothing—and he breathes in as if he's trying to summon it.

Tom's skin is thin, which can be both a blessing and a curse. He sleeps under 15 tog duvets in thirty-degree heat without breaking a sweat. He's practically translucent. You could see his heart swell and deflate as he waits and waits, but he's at his bravest in the rain. The drops freckling his face remind him that he has skin. He sees a dark figure dotting in and out of the streetlights, and he feels it, the welling-up inside of him and the need to hide it. She runs into him, head-to-toe in waterproofs, rustling into his arms like a dry autumn leaf.

'There are slugs everywhere,' she says. 'What's going on? Where's your coat?'

'I don't want a coat.'

'But you'll get soaked.' She unzips her coat and wraps what she can around his arms.

He pulls away. 'No I don't need it.'

'Why not?'

'Because, we are going to dance in the rain.' He picks up her hand and bows.

'What?'

'But you have to take off your coat too. And your over-trousers.'

'Really? Can't I just keep mine on?'

He remembers how his mother took his hands to dance in the puddles that popped with rain. He takes the sides of Hannah's open coat and repeats what his mother said to him: 'What's the point of dancing in the rain if you can't feel it?'

Hannah's gaze pools on him and she smiles like a gracious loser. He sweeps away her coat, showing her tanned-leather shoulders and her skin ripples. Droplets cling to Tom's arm hairs, turning them white so he appears more cloud than man. Each drop feels carefully crafted for her and it's cold, barely bearable, and she stands there for him until the rain crystallises on her skin, but she folds her arms to dam the sight. 'There's no music.'

'Yes there is,' he says. 'Listen.' He taps his foot three times, takes her hand, draws her close and holds her there until they feel the roaring inside of each other's chests. He whirls her out and streams crash like cymbals down the drains, beats fall from the avenue trees, clapping onto the pavement. Hannah lifts her head to taste the sky, and Tom's smile breaks the banks of his face and heart because he's been waiting in a drought for so long, but now, at last, the heavens had opened.

Is there life on Mars?

The stillness

'The end came swiftly. All over the world, their machines began to stop and fall. After all that men could do had failed, the Martians were destroyed and humanity was saved by the littlest things, which God, in His wisdom, had put upon this Earth.'

Your hallucinations stopped intermittently. When this happened, you were quizzed about your after-life options. Did you want to be downloaded and then uploaded to an AI? Even my Calling-Avatar couldn't filter my heartbreak when you said no.

You said you had always wanted to know what it would be like, away from matter. That you would always be wondering what if there was more than this world. What if there was another? 'Let them have my body,' you said. 'We're all for the eating.' And then you told me to open up the notebook you kept locked, and there, tucked inside, pressed and dried was my weapon – a single, red rose. The one I had picked to tell you the shape of my heart. And I could barely look at it, to see it flattened, shrivelled, lifeless. You smiled and looked at me, and I still couldn't say it. I thought that if I said it, you would go. You would have no need to stay. That the rose would fall apart in my hands.

Part Five

*'The truth is of course
is that there is no journey.
We are arriving and departing
all at the same time.'*

– David Bowie

Is there life on Mars?

'For neither do men live nor die in vain.'

When I plucked the scarlet rose I had wanted to tell you that I loved you in a way that could live up to yours. The first time you told me you loved me, you picked daisies from your garden and braided them into a necklace, hanging them around my neck.

'I made sure they're only Fibonacci numbers,' you said.

I squinted. 'Who's he? Do I need to be worried?'

You laughed and had to explain it to me – about the odd numbers. 'So there's no need to pluck the petals to find out if I love you,' you said.

You asked me what I believe happens after we die and I couldn't answer you. Not because I didn't know, but because words were too small for it now, too thin. Words were too fixed. They didn't expand or breathe like it, and I couldn't tell you how it spoke to me. How it brought you closer to me in daisies and curls, and how they grow around you and follow me, even now that you're gone. I could not tell you because I wasn't sure if it was real. If you were real.

But it was. It is. And I remember how you stared at me and said: 'Well, do you promise you'll wait around for me when we find out?' And I twisted the daisy chain necklace into a figure eight, and I told you 'Forever. I would wait forever.'

The last thing my father sang to me

There is a painting in my father's house that we would step into. My father would take my brother and I, prop us on his knee, and sing:

'Oh! You pretty things...'

We paddled in oils and canvas. We skimmed rocks on the lake to see them skip. We walked under white-nosed mountains and sailed on boats. We drank the blues like we were thirsty. We held the white snow as if it was cubes of ice on our brow. We rolled on the greens as if they were cushions for our backs.

The painting became our window when we were too afraid to look out of ours. It became our utopia, our haven. It was a door out of our house when we couldn't leave. My father would sit and stare into it for hours. When I asked him where he was and what he was doing, and whether I could join him, he would tell me that he was walking with God. That he must speak, from one father to another, alone.

My father decided we should leave our country when he came back with milk and bread. He was far away from us in a painting I did not know. He spoke closely to my mother in whispers. They hammered their decisions to the wall with nods. We packed and waited. I stared at the painting we could not take.

There were buses, camps, my father, my mother, my brother. I remember running. Walking. Hiding. Stepping on toes. Howls and explosions. My mother's gasp, how soft and quiet it was, but how crystal clear it echoed through me. How close it was. Her hand clenched mine as if it would never let go.

But it did.

When buildings fell, when people cried, when bodies became rubble, I went back into the painting, singing my father's favourite song. I went back to the lake with my father to feel golden rays blot on my face. When my parents did not get into the dinghy with us, I took their hands and walked under the oil mountains back towards home. When they became dots on the shore, I imagined it in reverse, them getting bigger, waving me back in, waving me home, calling me 'son'.

I did not sleep – I passed out. My father's carpentry

notebooks were my pillow. We'd left and arrived. We'd reached a new world. But it was not ours. I did not know it.

Utopia means nowhere, and this is where I am. I am nowhere. There's no more painting. And here is not where I am. It's not where I can be. It's a painting I cannot get into. I cannot paint myself into it. It's unfamiliar. Un – famil- iar. Un – family. I see remembered faces in new crowds. My old world haunts me. Misplaced. Mis-placed. Miss place. Miss my place. I have been placed, but missed.

When you break it down…

Break

down.

You see the parts. The missing parts. Family. Place.

And I am beginning to forget. Were there boats on the lake? Did my mother have a mole on the right or left of her nose? What pitch did my father sing at? Was he in tune? I do not know if the painting at my father's house still exists, or if the walls are all crumbs instead of bricks. Whether the dust in my town, on my street, will ever settle. Whether it still sticks to you, and paints your face as you walk through. The dust here is not on the streets. It got into their heads, into their looks, clouding their picture.

But I hear him, my father, in the brushstroke between sleeping and waking. I feel myself walking, a cool breeze swirling off a lake, and I hear his faint whistle, and then I remember.

Lifeline

I went for a black balloon. Bit of red and blue string. Reckoned it was apt, like a black star. The rubber squeaks no end though, and it feels cheap. Empty. Like something I'd give to baby Ally, because I wouldn't have to worry about her chewing the bejesus out of it.

So I bite the rubber opening between by teeth, blow to fill it with the words you gave me, to make it something worthwhile. But once I'd let it out, the balloon weighed heavy. A limp, un-watered, half-alive, freakish thing. It'll never reach you. It'll never get off the ground.

How on earth could I send this piece of shite up to you? It doesn't say what I want it to say. It says, 'here's a clichéd piece of crap, everything you hate, and *feeeeel* how much you mean to me.' God, I'm beyond bad at this. You were so good at it. Speaking to me. Being there for me. And here I am, with this gesture that's so pathetic, it's basically an insult.

This is, in no way, what I wanted to say.

But I don't have words. That's my problem. Only

moments. Memories. Stuff that's so tissue-deep and raw, that they've now fused to my bones. You gave me permission to be that girl in my Dad's old suits. No, it was way more than that – you made it feel extraordinary. Better than the rest. No norms. No lines.

You were my Jesus, my bible, my saviour, when they tried to pray me away. When my flaws became their mission, you showed me a rainbow in their black and white. That it was their sin, not mine, makin' hell. That I didn't need to keep living their rules. I didn't have to be a straight line. To keep drawing it over and over again on my wrists. I could be any shape I wanted.

No, I didn't have words for you. I only had flesh and bone. They are me. My very breath. And so I breathe, deep. So deep that it hurts. That I can feel it ripping into my ribs, into my fabric, into the parts of me I had healed over, that had scarred, so that you could hear them tear.

And I want to open them up for you. So you could know. And the balloon is fit to burst and it lifts me off the ground, and I wrap the string around my wrist, around the lines I drew on myself to keep me in, and I think how amazing it is that they have faded. The lines are almost gone, except one…

The one that's holding onto you.

But I don't want to let it go, because then it would be true. You wouldn't be here. You'd be gone. You'd be human. There would be no second coming.

But I needed you to know. To hear that ripping in me.

So I let go.

I let go.

And I hope. I hope it reaches you.

The man who sold the world

'You should go to the Man who sells the world, you can't miss him. Just down the road. He's building a boat out front. Lovely man,' said nosey-next-door Jan.

'I'll just get one from a shop,' I said.

'Oh nothing beats what he has. I don't know where he gets it from. But they're full of stories that Hoshi would love. I'll ask him if he has one.'

'Don't go to any trouble…'

'No trouble.' She sailed off down the street, as if she was on her way to do it right there and then. The next day she tells me to go there on the weekend and take a look at it.

I take Hoshi, more for me than her, and spot the house with a half-boat and clumps of soggy sawdust on the driveway. I rang the doorbell and waited. I rang again. In my peripheral, something moved in the front window. I rang again, knocked and shouted *Hello?*

The door opened 30° E to show a frowning man eating a crumpet. 'Yes?'

'Uh…'

'Dad, he looks just like you,' said Hoshi.

'Shhh, we're here about the globe?'

'Sorry, I don't have a globe.'

'But Jan said…' He began to close the door. 'My daughter…'

'Daughter?' He opened the door wider and it could have been a reflection if it wasn't for his cloudy beard.

'She wants to be an explorer. Isn't that right, Hoshi?'

'Does she now? What an ambitious profession. Where do you wish to go?' He kneeled down to her.

'Madagascar,' she said.

'What about Japan? It's beautiful there.'

Hoshi nodded, and I jumped to my defence. 'We haven't had a chance to take her…'

'Come on through. I might have something better.' He led us to the garden and over decking. He picked up an old, cracked head-torch, and lifted a trap door. He twisted and stepped down an old swimming pool ladder. 'In you come.'

I dived into a sea of castoffs and treasures and called Hoshi down once I'd checked it out. Ripples of light beamed through the gaps above, and we towed after him into the centre. His torchlight hooked onto a huge globe that glowed alone as if it were the sun and all the other pieces around were held in its orbit.

'Here it is little girl. My world.'

Hoshi ran toward it, and her face lit up in his beam. 'Wow.'

He spun it. 'My daughter was like you. Exploring. She brought back a bit of each place and put it in here.' He lifted up the top half and then closed it before we could see.

'What's in it?' asked Hoshi.

'You'll have to find out. Take it. It's yours.'

'No, we couldn't possibly. It belongs…'

'To no one. Take it, for her.'

'Oh please, Dad.'

His torch put his face in shadow so I couldn't see his expression to figure out what it meant to him. 'Okay. We'll take it. How much?'

'Tomorrow. I will bring it tomorrow. I will need to pully it out.'

***

The next day, I opened the door to Jan. 'Did you know there's a globe out here for you?'

'Is there?'

'He must have dropped it off just before.'

'Before what?'

'Did you not hear? Poor Tomo. He's in hospital. A bunch of his stuff collapsed on him. Made a big bang. Echoed through the street about an hour ago. Didn't you hear it? Bangs and sirens. Shook the earth, it did. Surprised you didn't feel it.'

'What a shame. I hope it wasn't our fault.'

'Yeah he's not been the same since his daughter disappeared.'

'What happened to her?'

'Went to hike up some mountain and vanished. Nobody could find her. Such a sad story. She was his entire world. Used to wait up for her to come back off some trip somewhere, working on that boat. Now…' She shrugged.

Hoshi jumped into the hallway. 'Did you say the globe was here?'

I moved to the side and she ran out, almost colliding with it. She started to lift the top of the globe and I wondered.

'Wait,' I said.

'What?'

'Let's not open it, not yet…'

You do not believe in ends

They said the world would end that day, but turns out t'was just the beginning. You was dead set against endings. You finished nothin'. Home was all exposed wires, doors propped up on walls waiting to be hinged, and dead lightbulbs, years old, that told us to evolve in the dark. But you was plenty-good at startin' something – fights and whatnot. You was always ready. Your t-shirts had no sleeves t'roll up – that's how ready you was. But I reckon you was a wuss about dying really, your tats of fire and skulls were all make-believe. Posing. You couldn't see no end.

That's why you drove us to the maze that weekend. Labyrinth, you said. There's a difference. All beginnings and starts, no ends. We stood ready at the get-set-marks of the three entrances, shaded by corn that had dried t'a crisp, and Darren and I whispered *maze* t'each other. But you heard and your eyes were bullet-holes, so we dared not say another word as Darren was still blue from crying on account of not being man-enough, and so on three, we ran on in, racing each other back to where we'd just been.

And as I ran and ran and ran, I wished you gone. I wished your end. I wished for Minotaurs and death, and the end of the world all in the middle of that dead ol'maze, and I couldn't figure why Mom made us say our prayers for you, because you do not believe in ends. You do not believe in conclusions, in facing up t'sins. In bein' responsible for what you done t'us.

And when I came out, back at the beginning, there was nobody there. I beat your ass. And I had a real moment; one that showed me that I was better than you, that you were not God nor King. You was weak, human. And I figured that at some point, some day, I could take you. You'd have t'face me. I'd be your end.

And they said the world would end that day, but t'was just the beginning.

ACKNOWLEDGEMENTS

To my heroes…

❮ Miss Mandy Ovens who lent me her home and therefore her heart. Here's to saving each other until the lights go out.

❮ Mark, his generous spirit and blind support, drive me forward – literally and figuratively.

❮ Yuki for her authenticity and not being annoyed at my constant attempts to save her.

❮ The two Kates in my life who showed up when others didn't, who have never wanted anything but to be friends, after all these years, all this time. The biggest mystery of all.

❮ My Nan for giving me a safety net, decades of unconditional love and Diet Coke.

❮ Mum and Dad, hero-veterans, for their boundless grace and help for a daughter with too many feelings.

❮ Zelda Chappell, advocate and gardener, who planted a seed that grew into these pages.

The Flash Mob, and the flash community for their understanding ears, inspiring stories and boundless support.

Tania Hershman whose friendship and wisdom stopped me from giving up on myself.

Ken Elkes who's picked me up (and my notebooks) when I left myself behind.

Amanda Saint who 'got it' and loved it, along with everyone who has published a story of mine, who have never tried to make me anything but who I am.

Gillian Best for bestowing me with lucky coins; Philippa – a champion to be championed; the Divorce Force and DARO.

Mike – for seeing me and whose very presence in my life has caused me to be every writer's worse nightmare: a cliché.

And finally to Bowie, his life and work, inspiring and singing to every part of my humanity. Thank you to everyone for believing, for giving me the courage to be me, in helping me to learn when to let go, and when to grab your hands and run with you.

Thanks to the following publishers where versions of these stories first appeared:

Swings and rocket ships, first published in *Bare Fiction* magazine in 2016.

You do not believe in ends, first published as 'Dead bulbs' in the *Brighton Prize Anthology 2017*.

If you've enjoyed these stories, you can read more from some of the writers featured here, plus many other talented authors, in other Retreat West Books.

WHAT WAS LEFT, VARIOUS

20 winning and shortlisted stories from the 2016 Retreat West Short Story and Flash Fiction Prizes. A past that comes back to haunt a woman when she feels she has no future. A man with no mind of his own living a life of clichés. A teenage girl band that maybe never was. A dying millionaire's bizarre tasks for the family hoping to get his money. A granddaughter losing the grandfather she loves. A list of things about Abraham Lincoln that reveal both sadness and ambition for a modern day schoolgirl.

AS IF I WERE A RIVER, AMANDA SAINT

Kate's life is falling apart. Her husband has vanished without a trace – just like her mother did. Laura's about to do something that will change her family's lives forever – but she can't stop herself. Una's been keeping secrets – but for how much longer?

NOTHING IS AS IT WAS, VARIOUS

A charity anthology of climate-fiction stories raising funds for the Earth Day Network. A schoolboy inspired by a conservation hero to do his bit; a mother trying to save her family and her farm from drought; a world that doesn't get dark anymore; and a city that lives in a tower slowly being taken over by the sea.

SEPARATED FROM THE SEA, AMANDA HUGGINS

Separated From the Sea is the debut short story collection from award-winning author, Amanda Huggins. Crossing oceans from Japan to New York and from England to Havana, these stories are filled with a sense of yearning, of loss, of not quite belonging, of not being sure that things are what you thought they were. They are stories imbued with pathos and irony, humour and hope.

IMPERMANENT FACTS, VARIOUS

These 20 stories are the winners in the 2017 Retreat West Short Story and Flash Fiction prizes. A woman ventures out into a marsh at night seeking answers about herself that she cannot find; a man enjoys the solitude when his wife goes away for a few days; two young women make a get rich quick plan; and a father longs for the daughter that has gone to teach English in Japan.

http://retreatwestbooks.com

Lightning Source UK Ltd.
Milton Keynes UK
UKHW020501020621
384753UK00006B/295